Our Song

A Country Music Novella

by
CASEY PEELER

A Country Music Novella
By Casey Peeler

Interior Formatting by Cassy Roop at Pink Ink Designs

Chapter One

As I hit the last note of my most current single, the crowd goes wild, and the stage goes dark. "Thank you, Charlotte! Now put your hands together for Jake Bryant!"

Exiting the stage, I glance over my shoulder into the crowd and cannot believe how my life has changed in the last six months. It wasn't long ago that I spent my weekends hitting up every local country bar within a hundred mile radius of Lattimore trying to make a name for myself. Little did I know that Cole, the manager of my favorite country bar, Coyote Joe's, had made sure that a certain country music god caught a glimpse of me at their amateur night.

Walking down the hall backstage, I come face-to-face with the country music god himself. "Don't worry, Belle. This never gets old. You do know that before long you're gonna be closing a show down."

"Thanks, Jake. But I'm just gonna enjoy this ride right now. I'll see ya from the crowd," I say with a wink.

Hurrying to my dressing room, I make a quick trip into the powder room, change into clothes a little less divaish and hurry back to find a spot in the crowd. I honestly think I could watch Jake Bryant every single night on that stage, and not just for the way that his ass looks in those jeans either. He has one of the best voices in country music today. It's like sweet honey to my ears, and I swear, it gets sweeter every time I hear it.

As I grab my water, I hear the voices of thousands of screaming fans, and with the first downbeat of his current number one hit, every word is being sung by Jake and the crowd. Gah! That's got to be the best feeling ever. I walk double time to make my way out into the crowd. Security knows exactly what I'm up to. Since the first day I began touring with Jake, once my set is over, I enjoy his show just like everyone else, directly in the pit. One perk is that I always get a good spot thanks to security.

As Jake slows it down, I laugh when he finds my eyes in the crowd and then winks. Of course, all the girls around me think it's for them, but I know that it's for me. The truth is, Jake Bryant has become my best friend since the day he signed me to his tour. He's the complete opposite of what I expected a country mega star to act like; he's a perfect gentleman. Maybe it's due to the close quarters we endure while traveling, but he is an absolute sweetheart, and I'll take that fine ass any day!

I sing along with the crowd to every song, sway my hips back and forth, and lift my drink at the appropriate times. When the next to the last song in the set begins, I make my way back out of the crowd and to the stage entrance. I finish watching the show from the side of the stage.

As Jake finishes his finale, he takes a bow and runs offstage toward me. He lifts me off the ground and spins me around.

"Glad to see me?" I ask.

"You have no idea what it's like to look out into the crowd and find eyes that you know. Really know, Belle."

"If I didn't know better, Mr. Bryant, I'd think somebody had a crush."

"If I didn't know better, I'd think you liked it."

"What can I say? I'm a sucker for a country boy in tight ass jeans that knows how to work a stage."

Jake puts me down, and we start to make our way to sign autographs. This makes for a long night, but at least we have a few days off before hitting the road again. The big man upstairs must have been looking out for me because I can go home for a few days. That means no tour bus, cameras, hotel rooms, or getting decked out to the nines every night. I get to see my family and friends, be myself, and enjoy life as a normal twenty-two year old.

"So, Jake, what have you got planned for your days off?"

"Well, I guess I'm gonna just stay on the bus. Why?"

"Well, I was thinkin'."

"Oh lord, you're thinkin'?" he asks as he stops and crosses his arms.

"Yeah, well, I was thinkin' about goin' home for a few days. I mean, it's like thirty minutes from here. Honestly, I can't believe more of my family and friends didn't show up tonight."

"Um, Belle. You might wanna turn around."

As I turn around, I'm met by everyone that is important to me— my parents, my brother Beau, and my friends Lyndsay and Chase from Coyote Joe's.

Lyndsay and I do the same squeal, dance in place, and then rush to each other. Chase and Beau laugh, and Mama and Daddy just shake their heads.

"Oh my gosh, y'all! I didn't even know y'all were here! I didn't see you in the seats I left for ya'll."

"Well, that's because Jake found us some a little closer." Spinning around, I find Jake and place my hands on my hips. "You pulled this stunt, Jake Bryant?"

Smiling, he answers, "Guilty."

"I freakin' love you!"

"Whoa now, Belle. Don't go droppin' a four-letter word over some concert tickets."

"Aw, hush! So, y'all wanna head to the bus? We have to sign a few autographs real quick."

"Sure, honey," Mama says. As they walk to the bus, Jake and I make our way to fifty screaming fans.

After we finish signing the last autograph and security whisks us away, I realize how tired I really am. I can't wait to see my family, but honestly, I just want a caramel coffee from Dunkin Donuts and my bed.

"I'll let you have some time with your family. What was it that you were gonna say earlier?"

"Oh, I was thinkin' 'bout goin' home for a few days or so. I just need a little groundin', ya know? I didn't know what you were planning, but thought if you were in need of some home cookin' and a real bed you might wanna come, too."

Jake stops, and I turn to face him.

"If you can promise me that I won't have a million teenage girls after me, we have a deal."

"Well, I can make that promise because there aren't more than a couple hundred teenagers total in Lattimore."

"You should be a damn comedian, ya know?"

"I'll keep that in mind if this gig doesn't work out," I say as I walk up the stairs to my bus.

"Just be ready in the morning, and we will head that way."

"Aight." He turns and walks to his bigger mansion of a bus.

Chapter Two

Once I reach the top step onto my bus, Lyndsay hounds me. "Did I just hear that right? Jake Bryant is comin' to Lattimore?"

"Yes, but if you so much as post it on any social media site, I'll kill you! You got it?"

"Easy, killer," Chase says.

I give Chase a WTH look, and he gives me one right back. That is why he is my favorite bouncer at Joe's. He keeps it real and looks out for me at the same time.

"Well, I just don't want a million screamin' girls going goo-goo for Jake Bryant while we're trying to enjoy a break."

"Please tell me that y'all aren't dating?" my mama asks. She has never been one to sugar coat anything.

"No, Mama! We aren't dating, sleeping, or doing anything together. We are just friends, and I plan on keepin' it that way."

Beau almost chokes on his beer at my comment. He's always loved how I tell it like it is, and he's always trying to keep things quiet around our parents. Leave it to me to spill every party being thrown in Lattimore, who was dating whom, cheatin' on whom, or anything else that happens in a small town. I'm sure that being the older brother he is, he was probably ready to kill me six out of seven days a week.

"Good to know," Daddy says. "Well, I guess that means we need to get home and make sure things are ready for not one, but two, big stars to come to town."

"Daddy! There ain't nothin' special about us. We just got lucky, that's all."

"Oh, there's plenty special about you, sweetheart, and don't you forget it."

Mama, Daddy, and Beau go home while Lyndsay and Chase hang around for a little while longer. We brew a pot of coffee, sit, talk, and enjoy a night like we used to every Friday night after Joe's closed. I love these two, and honestly, every day is hard because they aren't a part of my life like they used to be.

As the clock approaches four in the morning, they stand to leave, but I can't let them drive at this time of night.

"Y'all just stay. I'm leavin' in the mornin'. It's late, and I've missed y'all," I tell them.

Lyndsay looks at Chase. "Whatever you wanna do, Lynds," he says.

"Well, I've never stayed on a famous country star's tour bus before, so hell to tha yeah!" she exclaims.

I loan Lyndsay some pajamas, and we get ready to watch a little TV before going to bed. Within ten minutes, Lyndsay is ready to call it a night, and I tell her to take my bed. She doesn't argue and shuts the door behind her. Chase and I finish watching Grown Ups, or should I say, attempt to watch it. Before I know it, the sun is rising, and I'm snuggled into the crook of his arm. Shit!

Trying my best not to wake him, I attempt to slide away as he begins to mumble something that I can't understand. Then, his arm starts to squeeze me like a boa constrictor. That's when I realize he's no longer asleep and just being the ass that I love.

"I can't breathe, Chase! Let me go!"

"I'll let you go when you scream to the world that I am best man on Earth."

Without thinking, I do exactly that. I yell those words, and Lyndsay pushes open the door like the smoke alarm just sounded. Her hair is all kinda crazy. "What the hell was that?" she asks.

"Oh, you know. It's just me professing how Chase is the best man on Earth, because if I don't, he will squeeze all the air outta my lungs."

"Lord, can y'all fall in love already?" She turns around and returns to bed.

Chase and I look at each other like she's lost her damn mind. That's one thing I know about Chase and me. We are just friends. He's been there since the first day I walked into Joe's, and he's always stayed. When I needed a dance partner, he was there. When I needed a drinking buddy, he was there, and when I just needed a friend, he was there. Chase is my constant.

Chase finally lets go of his death grip, as there is a knock at the door. I make my way over and open it. Jake Bryant is there, packed and ready to go to my hometown. Who would have ever thought that I'd take a country music star home to the podunk town of Lattimore?

"Hey, Jake. Come on up."

Once he's on the bus, he has a confused look when he notices both Chase and me still in our clothes from last night.

"Chase and Lyndsay stayed last night."

"Well, I hate I missed the party," he says as he eyes Chase.

I just shake my head. Give me ten minutes, and we'll be on the road.

Hurrying into my room, I tell Lyndsay to get moving and also inform her that the country god is on the bus. I've never seen a girl move so fast in my life.

"What?" she asks.

"Um, he's just a guy."

"To you, maybe, but I'm no dummy. I see the way he looks at you. In fact, if I were you, I'd act on that if I had the chance."

As I stuff some clothes into my bag, I answer her, "I can't go there. Do you know what will happen to this tour if we go there?"

"Belle it's only for three more months. Then after that, you know you're going to get asked to headline."

"I don't know about that, but if so, it would make things weird. And I don't do weird."

Lyndsay drops it, and we make our way to the living area. Chase and Jake seem to be engaged an in-depth conversation. They both look like they are ready to throw blows at each other.

"Everyone ready to go?" I ask to relieve the tension. "Chase and Lynds, Jake and I will follow y'all." I have to say that it's nice that he has his truck handy, because I honestly hadn't thought that part through. I guess I would have ridden home with Chase and Lyndsay or called Beau to pick me up.

As Jake's diesel engine hits the highway, he turns down the radio. "What can I expect in this place called Lattimore?"

"Well, it's like any other redneck town. Everyone knows your business. We have the best burgers this side of I-85, a pool hall, and let's just say, we know how to get down on the farm."

"Nice. Sounds exactly like where I want to spend my break. Do Chase and Lyndsay live there, too?"

"Yeah, I've grown up with them, but we all started really hangin' out when we were old enough to go to Joe's. It's in Charlotte. We learned every country line dance, partied hard on 1-2-3 nights, and when amateur nights started, they put my ass up on stage and that's been all she wrote."

"I played there when I first got signed. You know that's what people do, right? They play the small country nightclubs from city to city and hope and pray the fans love them."

"I know. I do believe that I saw a Jake Bryant there not so long ago," I say with a smirk. "I've seen anyone from Florida Georgia Line to Blake Shelton there. That was always the plus of Lyndsay and Chase workin' at Joe's. I always got to meet people, and they were normal, just like you and me."

"Now, how did I manage not to meet you when I played there?"

"Probably because you wouldn't have noticed me with the groupies all over you."

"That has to be the worst part. You know most guys would kill to be in my spot, but I just want someone to like me for me, not because I'm this country music god that you say I am."

"I won't say that I didn't have a total fangirl moment once I realized I'd be touring with you. Well, actually both Lynds and I did. Chase laughed his ass off at us that night, but then I was over it. I realized we are professionals, and we need to keep it that way."

The inside of the truck is quiet for a few minutes, and then Jake finally breaks the silence.

"I'm thankful they got you up on that stage, Belle. I was there that night. When you started singin', I knew I had to have you on tour with me. You were a voice to remember and not so bad to look at either," he says with a wink.

Holy crap! Did he really just hit on me? I swear I just used the word 'professional' in my last comment, and now he's flirting.

"Well, I love music. I always have, and there is just something about connecting with people because your song touched their heart."

"Can I ask you one more thing?"

"Shoot," I say.

"What's really going on with you and Chase? It's none of my business, but I see the way he looks at you."

"Nothing. He's my friend."

"Right, if you say so."

"Why does everyone have that same reaction?" I question as we stop at the only stoplight in Lattimore. Jake turns toward me.

"Because I see the way he looks at you, and if you want me to be honest, I look at you the same way. I know you want to keep this relationship professional, but I'm not makin' any promises."

Completely floored. That is what I am. Maybe bringing Jake Bryant home isn't a good idea, because as much as I want to say that it needs to stay professional, I know deep down that I want a little bit of what's in those jeans.

Chapter Three

A s we pull up to the two-story brick house on seventy-five acres, I see the wheels turning in Jake's mind.

"Whatcha thinkin'?" I ask.

"I think this is beautiful. You described a rinky-dink town, and this house isn't rinky-dink. Do y'all own all this land?"

"Yup. It's been in the family for years. You see that little farm house right there?" I point out the window to the right. "That's my mawmaw and pawpaw's. They bought this when my pawpaw came home from the war. He always wanted his own farm like his dad but bigger, and that's what he got. Daddy loved it just as much and decided to build on the land and run the farm with him. We sell cotton to all the local factories within the southeast."

"In other words, people know exactly who y'all are in town," he responds.

"No, it's not like that here. Lattimore is a tight-knit community. We all work together, and my family provides a lot of jobs for people in town. We aren't the biggest farm in town, if that's what you're wondering."

Pulling up to the house, Jake puts the truck in park. He is in complete awe, and it totally throws me off guard. What is his deal?

His house outside of Nashville is a mansion, but for some reason, he's blown away by a farm in podunk Lattimore.

"Jake, it's just a house that cotton built. There's nothing fancy here. I promise once you walk through those doors, you will feel at home. My mama ain't the best housekeeper, but she can cook. Daddy works from sun up to sun down, and Beau, well, that's another story. He's tried his best to make it outta here, but for some reason, he keeps getting pulled right back in."

"I'm sorry. It's just that I didn't expect this."

"What'd you expect? A single wide?"

"Um, maybe," he says with a laugh.

I do believe this is the first time that he has ever pissed me off. "Back up, Jack. First off, let me tell you that if I lived in a cardboard box, I'd still be proud if it was all my daddy could afford. Secondly, what gave you the idea I was trailer trash?"

Jake is dumbfounded because I have never spoken like that to him, but he has struck a nerve.

He slides closer to me, and my breathing stops for a moment.

"Belle, I didn't mean that. The way you talk about this town is like there is nothing great about it, but since we hit the county line, I've been amazed by what I've seen. I wish I'd grown up in a place like this. My childhood was spent going from one military base to another. I've never had a real home. I'm sorry if I offended you."

With one comment, that's all it takes for me to get off my high horse and return to normal.

"What did you mean when you said Beau was 'another story'?"

"He loves music too, but I'm the one that made it out, and he's still here. He and I used to write together all the time, but what he's really good at is making a set a reality."

Breaking our connection, I tell him, "Come on. Let's get inside." That's enough about Beau for now. I grab his hand and pull him toward the front porch.

As we enter the house, the aroma of Sundrop Pound Cake hits my nostrils. Mama is doing what she does best. Cooking. I can't wait to have a piece with a glass of milk.

"Hey, Mama. We're here!" I yell as I close the door behind us. She comes to greet us in the foyer, and Beau is in the living room. He doesn't get up; he just gives a wave and goes back to watching his hunting show. You'd think that he'd notice I'm home. Oh, well.

"Hey, Beau! Don't get up or anything," I say just a little bit on the sarcastic side.

"Belle, I'll have something sweet for ya in a few minutes. Why don't you take Jake to the guest room so he can get settled?"

"Yes, ma'am."

Jake and I make our way upstairs and down the hall. He stops to look at the family photos on the wall and asks me questions about all of them. Please don't ask about the one where my hair is half-brushed, and I look like I have rotten teeth because I didn't pull a loose tooth. Whew! Made it past it! I give him a brief tour as we make our way to the guest room.

"Here ya go, Jake," I say as I open the guest room. "Mine's right next door if ya need anything." Stupid, Belle. Stupid comment. "I'm gonna go get settled. I'll be right back," I tell him.

I walk into my room and close my eyes as my back brushes the back of the door. What the hell was I thinking bringing home the country music god? He's perfect in every single way. His eyes, hair, perfectly sun-kissed skin, impeccable ass in a pair of jeans, and a personality to go with it, but the fact that he likes me for me is the biggest turn-on ever.

I walk to my dresser and look in the mirror. Touching up my makeup, I decide that it's time to show Jake what it's like in Lattimore. I send Chase and Lyndsay a text.

Group Text:

Me: Martin's tonight? Time to show Mr. Country Music God how we do it in Lattimore. Y'all in?

Chase: Sure, Beau coming 2?

Me: Prob

Lyndsay: Damn right! I'll spread the word.

Me: Don't you dare! Let's just see who's out tonight. Meet us there at 8.

As I place my phone down, there's a light knock at my door.

"Come in." Turning around, I see him. "You ready for the best cake you've ever eaten? Then, I think you need a tour of the farm."

"I'm game."

We make our way into the kitchen and take a seat. Mama has the cake, butter, and glasses of milk waiting. Beau has beaten us to the table already. I should have known. We each grab a piece, slather it with butter, and take a bite.

"Wow." Is the only word that Jake says with a mouthful of cake. Lawd knows what I'd love him to have a mouthful of!

As we eat our cake, I tell Beau and Jake the plans for tonight. Beau gives me a questioning glance, and I give him a go to hell look. He says that he will be bringing his girlfriend, Sarah, and will just meet us there. That's odd. I swear I've got to tell him my thoughts about making it big before I leave.

Once we finish eating, I excuse Jake and myself. It is a beautiful Carolina summer day, and it's time to show Jake why there's no place like Carolina.

As we approach the barn, I give him the choice of Gator or four-wheeler. He chooses four-wheeler. This is going to be a blast.

We take off from the barn and go toward the edge of the property. I point out all the farm animals, the different barns, and then head toward my grandparents. We park the four-wheelers and then make our way inside my grandparents' quaint, old farmhouse that has been there since this farm was established.

"Mawmaw! Pawpaw!" I yell as we enter the side entrance of their house.

"Belle, is that you?" Mawmaw calls from her sewing room.

"Yes, ma'am!"

Before we are halfway to the room, Mawmaw is hurrying to meet me, but she stops abruptly when she realizes I'm not alone.

'Well, Belle, who do we have here?"

"Mawmaw, I'd like you to meet the country music god himself, Jake Bryant."

Jake's face turns red as a beet. It has to be the cutest thing I've ever seen.

"Nice to finally meet the guy who stole our little girl away. Do you know we saw her every day of her life until she went on the road with you?"

"No, ma'am. I didn't. I do apologize for that, but have you heard her sing? It'd be a shame not to share that voice with the world."

"That, Mr. Bryant, better not be some line you feed to a pond of fish because I've heard her sing since before she could talk."

"No, ma'am. It's not a line, but I'm pretty sure the fish are bitin' hook, line, and sinker when she's on stage."

Mawmaw looks at me, puts her hand on her hip, and says, "I like him! Never thought I'd say that one, but Mr. Country Music God just might be a keeper." And with that comment, she makes her way to the kitchen, and we follow after I pick myself up from the floor from embarrassment. We spend the next hour talking to her and Pawpaw about what it's like on the road. Jake talks about growing up in a military family, and of course, she tries to feed us.

It's early afternoon, and the sun is high in the sky. "Hey, Jake. I've got an idea. Come on."

We rev up the four-wheelers, and I put mine in high gear as we make our way to the creek. I haven't been out here in six months, and it is one of my favorite places on Earth... other than the stage.

Jake struggles to keep up with me. I stop when we reach the bank, and he almost plows into me.

"Easy there! Had a hard time keepin' up I see."

"Damn, I didn't know where the hell you were planning on going. I'm new here, remember?"

"Come on. Make sure you leave your phone up here."

Jake looks at me like he knows I'm up to no good. I take him by the hand, and he follows me to my own slice of heaven in the middle of nowhere.

We climb over the rocks to get to the other side of the creek and then walk for about a hundred yards before reaching the water hole.

"Belle, what are we about to do?" Jake asks unsurely.

"We are about to enjoy this beautiful summer Carolina day the best way I know how."

"And how's that?"

"In the water, duh?" Kicking off my shoes, I grab the rope swing and run straight for the water, screaming the entire way down.

Once I surface, Jake is standing there with his arms crossed.

"Are you comin' or what?" I ask.

Before I have time to process it, Jake is removing his T-shirt in one single motion. Hot-oh-mighty. With all the time we've been together, I can honestly say this is the first time I've seen him shirtless. God sure knew what He was doing when He created that boy. But, Jake doesn't stop there; next, he removes his boots and then his damn jeans. Jake Bryant is standing there in nothing but a pair of plaid boxers. I definitely didn't think this part through. He grabs the rope swing and jumps straight for me. I duck under the water to avoid the splash.

When we both surface, it's very evident that this has just crossed a line. Jake moves closer, wraps his arm around me, and pulls me to his body. My heart begins to beat out of my chest as he peers into my eyes.

"You promise me that there's nothing going on with you and Chase?"

"I promise."

That's all the reassurance that Jake needs as his lips get within inches of mine.

"You know this will change things. Don't you, Jake?"

"I'm ready for a change, Belle," he says as his lips crash into mine.

Jake pulls me closer to the bank without letting our lips lose contact. Once we are at the bank, his hands move all over my body with a hunger that I've never felt before. Everything inside me is saying this is a great idea, but my head is screaming for us to stop. Screw it; I'll clean up this mess later.

I let my hands run through his short brown hair and lose myself in him. We get lost in each other for what feels like an eternity.

As Jake begins to remove my tank top, I pull away slowly. It's my reality check.

"Um, Jake. I think we need to slow down. I mean, I don't know. This is happening so fast, and I don't want you to think that this is all I want."

Jake takes my hair and places it behind my ear as he gazes into my eyes. He smiles and moves in to graze my lips again.

"Belle, this was bound to happen. I'm just glad it happened here instead of out on the road. This place feels real, just like you."

"But you know this isn't a good idea."

"I'm willing to pay the price if you're willing to go along for the ride."

I've never been one to live in the moment. I always weigh all my options, but there's a first time for everything.

"Jake Bryant, you better not hurt me. Do you understand?"

He doesn't answer; he just attacks my lips again to seal the deal.

We make our way out of the water, and Jake slides his clothes back on as I drip dry. Once we are back at the four-wheelers, I stop him.

"I just told everyone last night that we are strictly professional. You know this is gonna make me look like I'm a liar."

"Then, let's not tell them."

"Jake, I don't know if you've realized it, but I'm pretty much an open book around my family. The moment I stop talkin' is the moment they know I'm full of shit."

"Well, don't stop talkin', and we can just try to keep this to ourselves until we are back on the road."

"You're gonna get me in so much trouble," I say as I close our distance and leave him with a kiss that will have him wanting more. I back away, crank up the four-wheeler, and take off. He knows my game this time and catches up quickly.

Once we get back, things feel a little awkward as we try to deny what just happened. We make our way back inside the house and upstairs to take showers and get ready for a night out in Lattimore. I know this is gonna be one for the history books.

As soon as I'm in my room, I turn on Pandora, start my shower, remove my wet clothes, and wrap a towel around me as I pick out something to wear tonight. There is a light knock at the door again. I assume it's Mama and tell her to come in. I quickly realize it's Jake.

As he opens the door and catches me in a towel, his mouth falls to the floor. "I'm sorry, Belle. I just didn't know where the towels were." I think about handing him mine, but realize that is a bad idea. My mama, brother, and daddy are downstairs.

"Oh, hold on. As I turn around to go to my bathroom to get him one, I'm stopped by the country music god within inches of my body.

"We could share you know."

Biting my lip, I reply, "I know, but I don't think that's a good idea. I mean, we just crossed this line, and you think I'm gonna get naked with you?"

"Belle, we've been tryin' not to cross this line since the day you started on tour, but I'll let you off the hook this time."

"Okay. Thanks, Jake," I say as I drop my towel and step into the shower. I can't help but giggle as I hear him exhale a deep breath.

"Belle, you better not laugh any more, or I'm coming in there."

With every ounce of my being, I try my best not to giggle, but the faintest sound comes out of my mouth. I attempt to cover my mouth, but it's too late. The shower curtain opens, and Jake enters clothes and all. He grabs the back of my neck, and his lips meet mine. The fire within them continues to get hotter and hotter as he backs me against the shower wall as the shampoo falls into the tub, and a moan escapes my mouth. Then, as if a light switch has been cut off, he pulls away, steps out, closes the curtain, and shuts the bathroom door.

It takes me a few minutes to wrap my mind around what just happened, but if I think this through, I know that I just lost at my own game. The ball is definitely in his court right now. He left me wanting nothing more than to give him every ounce of my being right there in the shower with my parents only feet away.

Chapter Four

Ohmygosh! Did that really just happen? I replay the events that occurred in this bathroom and shower. Yes, it did! Hot-oh-mighty! Cheesing like a schoolgirl, I give myself a pep talk. It's just Jake Bryant. OMG! Jake Bryant!!! Get it together, Belle! He's just another guy. Standing in the shower, I don't move until the temperature turns cold. Once I turn off the water, I step out and try to process how in the hell I'm gonna walk out of the room with a straight face when all I really want to do is jump into Jake's arms.

Shaking the thoughts from my mind, I decide to focus on the task at hand. What am I going to wear tonight? I can't overdo it because it's just Martin's, but I definitely want to make Jake sweat all night long. Glancing in my closet, I choose a pair of Rock n Roll Cowgirl jeans and a fitted hot pink tank top. For kicks, I grab a matching bra and panties, because the way things are going, who knows what bed I'll end up in tonight.

The music is still playing in the background as I begin to do my makeup and hair. As the song ends, that's when I hear the first beat to my newly released song, "Some Kinda Heartbreak." I drop my blush and scream to the top of my lungs. My door swings open, and Mama, Beau, and Jake are all standing there as if they are about to enter a crime scene.

"OHMYGOWD! Y'all, that's my song!"

Mama and I start singing while Beau stands there with a proud smile plastered on his face. It makes me smile even more that my big brother is happy for me because sometimes it is questionable. Mama takes advantage of the moment as she seizes him into her arms and dances with her baby boy while Jake takes the towel and briefly dries his hair. Then, he approaches me, still damp from the shower and shirtless. My, oh my! I have died and gone to country girl heaven! He asks for my hand, and we dance like no one is watching to my song in my bedroom. Jake takes a moment to surprise me by singing the words into my ear. "You're some kinda heartbreak, the kinda mistake, that I want to hold on to…" As I gaze up into those eyes, my heart melts.

When the song ends, we are brought back to reality. Jake winks at me and steps away, just like he would have done if it were this time yesterday. Mama gives me a hug, and I finish getting ready for Martin's. Lord knows it's gonna be a long night if we have to play it cool because we are anything but cool.

Chapter Five

Mama insists that we eat supper before going to the pool hall. We all come together at the table—Mama, Daddy, Beau, my grandparents, Jake and I. Mama has outdone herself again with fried chicken, mashed potatoes, corn, green beans, and homemade biscuits. Mawmaw brought her famous peach cobbler, and we are stuffed by the time it's over.

We take a few extra minutes to enjoy their company, which is something that we don't have often on the road. Jake takes every chance he can to brush the side of my leg with his hand, and it is driving me crazy. The sooner we get out of here the better.

I excuse Jake and myself from supper, and we make our way to the truck. He catches me off guard by opening the door and helping me inside before heading to the driver's side. Once he closes the door, he looks my way and smiles that perfect, up to no good, but I like it, grin.

"Belle, come here." I do as he asks and slide closer to him. Laying my head on his shoulder, I realize that I could get used to this, especially on the road. To know that I have someone at every stop would be amazing, but if I'm being real, I just don't know how this is going to work when we go back on tour.

Within minutes, we are at Martin's Pool Hall, and not one thing has changed. Chase's truck is here along with Lyndsay's car. Glancing around, I recognize a few other cars, including the bartender's.

"Come on. Let me show you how it's done in Lattimore," I say as I slide out the passenger side.

As I open the screen door, the smell of stale beer and cigarettes tickle my nose. Jerry is in his usual spot behind the bar. He whistles when I walk through the door. Leaving Jake at the entrance, I run to Jerry, throwing my arms around his neck. I can't believe I'm actually home.

After spinning me around, Jerry puts me down. I introduce Jake to him and the other locals. Chase has a pool table set and ready to go. We order a round of beers and crank up the jukebox with our favorite country songs before choosing teams based on our scientific method of rock, paper, scissors. Jake and Lyndsay are paired along with Chase and me.

After the second game, it's very evident that Jake got the bad end of the stick on this one. Lyndsay is definitely not the best at pool, and Chase and I are a team that's been playing together for the past five years.

Realizing that this isn't quite fair, we decide to play boys against girls, and the girls get beat easily.

Jerry keeps the beers coming, and by number five, I'm starting to feel the effects. The jukebox begins to play Tim McGraw and Faith Hill's "It's Your Love," and as if we are at Joe's, Chase wraps me in his arms and we dance in the middle of Martin's with all eyes on us, including Jake's.

Chase and I sing every word to each other and exaggerate our emotions. As the song comes to an end, Chase kisses the top of my forehead, and we go back to drinking our beer.

"Y'all do that often?" Jake asks with a hint of jealousy.

"That's our song," Chase says with territory in his voice.

"Of all songs, that's y'alls?" Jake questions.

"That's been our song ever since we started going to Joe's. They always play it there, and it's kinda our thing. I can remember one time this guy was trying his damnedest to get me to dance with him, and I was trying to explain that I couldn't. The next thing I knew Chase and his bouncer self showed up, and the guy ran off," I say as Chase smiles at me.

Jake takes a long pull on his beer, but his eyes never leave mine. For some reason, he's acting like I've done something wrong, but I'm not sure what.

"So, tomorrow's Friday. Do y'all have to work at Joe's?" I ask Chase and Lyndsay, not like I don't already know the answer.

"But, of course!" Lyndsay says and then has an OMG moment. "Y'all should totally come! I swear I won't tell a soul. It would be awesome. I bet people won't even recognize y'all. Oh, hell, who am I kidding? You know they will, but come on! Pleeeeaaasssssssseeeee?!" she begs.

As I look at Chase for guidance, he smiles. "I'm game if Jake is. He's the one that's gonna have to fight the girls off."

Chase chimes in on time as usual, "I hate to break it to ya, but Belle, you've grown up there. Cole is gonna end up doing something big once you get there. You know that, right?"

"He better not," I say with my hands on my hips. I know that it's gonna happen, and that we are both gonna end up on stage tomorrow night.

Knowing that the night is coming to an end, I glance at Chase and Lyndsay. They know exactly what I'm thinking.

"No way. Not tonight, Bella Blu," Chase says.

I just smirk, look at them and say, "Last one there has to jump first!" I grab Jake by the arm and run out of Martin's. Jerry is laughing his ass off behind the bar because he knows exactly what's up. We're going to the trestle.

Bursting through the door, I tell Jake to fork over his keys. He pauses, and I inform him we don't have time for this. He tosses me the keys, and we hurry to the truck. By the time we hit the main road, Chase is out in front. Damn.

"Do you care to explain this craziness? Or do I just have to wait till we get there?"

"When Beau was in high school, I used to follow him and his friends out here to the train trestle. He'd get so mad. I think he thought one of them might try to make a move or somethin'. They'd take a few beers and just chill on the tracks. It's hardly ever used anymore, so it's like an escape from reality. Then, I started going there to write, and one day Chase followed me. I gave him a bullshit story that this was my spot, and if he wanted to stay, he'd have to jump. Well, he did. So, we decided from that point on, the last one there has to jump. We pretty much just hang out, shoot the shit, get drunk, and jump. Every now and then we have to outrun a train, but those are few and far between."

"You're fuckin' kiddin', right?"

"That would be a no. I'm serious as a heart attack."

"Damn. Please make sure we aren't last. I've jumped one time already today, but knowing you're not waiting at the bottom makes this one less appealing."

"Who knows, I might jump with ya!" I wink.

As we pull up to the stoplight, I gun it to pass Chase, and Jake shoots him a bird. Mature I know. We are out in the lead, and within another five minutes, we'll be there. As we approach the trestle, I give Jake a play-by-play of the fastest route to the middle. As the headlights hit the parking spots, I realize that Lyndsay has somehow beaten us here.

"Well, damn. Looks like we're gonna have to haul ass if you don't want to jump." I throw the truck in park, and we sprint to the trestle. Chase is right behind us, and I know it's gonna be close. Chase runs past me and closes the gap on Jake. Once he's past him, Jake slows his sprinting to a jog until I catch up.

"Just so you know, I wasn't gonna let you jump alone," he says.

"Well, I'm a big girl, and there's nothing like the rush you get when you jump. I can promise ya that." And with that statement, I take off, leaving Jake in the dust.

We are all huffing and puffing at the trestle when Jake arrives. "That was so wrong, Belle. So wrong."

"What can I say? You fell for it, Mr. Country Music God, but if you want me to, I'll jump with ya."

Lyndsay and Chase look at each other. "That ain't in the rules, and you know it!" Lyndsay says.

"Rules are meant to be broken, and sometimes they are worth it," I say as I turn toward Jake.

As we make our way to the middle of the trestle, we reminisce about the last time we were here. It was the night I found out about the tour. Lyndsay, Chase, and I came out here to celebrate, and I put on a private concert for the two of them. We drank a case of beer, and then Lynds got a call from her boyfriend at the time. She ditched us, and Chase and I had the best night of our lives…. alone.

Chase and I have always been friends, but that night almost crossed the line. We don't talk about it, but as much as I try to deny that he has feelings for me, I know that Jake is right. He does, but I just can't go there. He's my best friend, and I can't mess that up. If that relationship ended badly, I'd never forgive myself. I pull myself from those thoughts, and notice that Chase is looking at me. He's thinking the same thing. Lyndsay and Jake are both oblivious to our exchange of glances and engaged in their own conversation.

Once we reach the middle, it's do or die for Jake.

"Aight, country music god. Let's see ya do it," I say.

"Y'all are really gonna make me do this?" We all nod in agreement.

"Aight, let me remove all forms of technology," he says as he removes his phone and all the contents from the pockets of his jeans. It's almost a replay of earlier today, and I look at Lyndsay who is totally drooling. I nudge Chase, and he laughs at her.

"What?" she asks. "Chase, you can't possibly tell me that if Carrie Underwood were standin' here right now, you wouldn't have to pick up your mouth off the ground."

"See somethin' you like?" Jake asks Lyndsay.

Standing with the confidence that only she can possess, she replies, "Damn right I do!"

"Aight, quit putting off the inevitable and jump already!" I say.

Jake makes his way to the edge of the trestle and peers over. "Y'all sure this water is deep enough?" I can see the worry on his face.

"Yes!" we yell.

"But if you want me to, I'll jump with ya, regardless of the rules," I say while removing my shoes and emptying my pockets. Not giving him a chance to respond, I grab his hand, count to three, and we jump off the top of the trestle into the river below.

As soon as our feet leave the track, my adrenaline increases, and it is pure bliss as we make our way into the water. Jake never lets go of my hand, and when we surface, he lets out a holler.

"That was amazing," he tells me as he stares into my eyes. "Just like you."

Not giving him a chance to make a move in front of Chase and Lyndsay, I pull him to the bank where things are a little more private before giving him permission to finish what he started in the water.

Understanding exactly what I'm doing, Jake takes me into his muscular arms and brings my lips to his. His hands begin to roam my body, and everything inside me heats up. It's very evident that he feels the same way.

As the heat increases to the point of combustion, I hear Chase holler for us. "Y'all comin'?"

I unwillingly pull away from Jake and answer, "On our way!" Then, he pulls me in for one more sizzling kiss.

Once we are back at the trestle, I see Chase and Lyndsay seated on the edge of the track talking in-depth about something, and if I have to guess, it has to do with Jake and me. Chase and his damn overprotective self.

Hearing us approach, Chase says, "'Bout damn time!"

"What? Are you mad I won't ever jump with you?" I ask with my hands on my hips.

"Never mind. Just get your ass over here before Lynds and I start arguing."

I shake my head and smile. They fight like brother and sister. Jake and I make our way to the middle and have a seat. Chase gets a case of beer from the truck, and we all pass them down and pop a top.

Without saying a word, we each take a long pull and sit there quietly. I can hear the water moving below, the hot summer breeze blowing through the trees, and the sound of crickets surrounding us. This is the perfect way to end a great night. Feeling that someone is staring at me, I glance to my right, and sure enough, Jake has those baby blues right on me. I smile back and take another swig of my beer.

"So, Belle, do you think you'll ever come back home for good?" Lyndsay asks.

I search my heart and soul for the answer. "I love Lattimore, but I don't think I'll ever come back home for good. I mean, I'd love to, but it doesn't look like it's in the cards for me. It's kinda funny how Beau is dying to get out, and I'd love to stay here forever."

Chase doesn't say a word as he crushes his beer can, tosses it into the water and begins to walk toward the other side of the track. Lyndsay motions for me to go see what the hell is his problem.

"I'll be right back," I tell Jake. Getting up, I finish my beer and grab two more before going that way.

I don't holler at Chase to stop; instead, I walk to catch up with him. Chase isn't one of many words, and whatever is bothering him must be pretty big for him to walk off like that. As my feet leave the track, I can see he's sitting on an old pine stump.

Once I reach him, I hand him another beer and have a seat beside him. We open our cans and just drink for a minute.

"Chase…" I start to say as he interrupts me.

"Don't, Bella Blu. Just don't," he pleads with hurt in his voice.

So I don't. I don't say it. I don't tell him that I wish he could go with me, that I hate not seeing Lyndsay and him every day, and how I wish there was a way for me to have the best of both worlds.

Instead, I take another drink of my beer, look at him, and turn off my emotions. "Chase, what do you want me to do? I can't believe you're acting like this. It's not like I can change my life. This is all I've ever wanted."

Glaring at me, he shakes his head. "Tell me, Bella Blu. Does he make you happy?" With a deer in the headlights look, I'm speechless. "That's what I thought. When he hurts you, I can't promise I'll be here to pick up the pieces," he says as he stands to leave, and then we feel it. The shaking of the earth below us. We look at each other and run as fast as we can to the trestle.

As we get on the trestle, we hear the sound of the whistle. It's coming; the train is coming. Lyndsay and Jake are sitting in the middle as I start to run toward them and yell for them to run. Chase takes me by the arm and stops me from running toward them.

"Train! Y'all run!" I shout a heart-wrenching scream as he pulls me to safety.

"Chase! Let me go! We can't just stand here and watch," I say as tears form inside my eyes.

"Yes, we can, and we will. I'm not letting you go."

Fear consumes my body as I watch Jake and Lyndsay run hand in hand across the track. They should just jump. Why didn't I say that? I can see the headlight of the approaching train, and tears begin to stream down my cheeks. No longer able to see Jake and Lyndsay, I turn and face into Chase's chest as a sob escapes my lungs. He places his hands in my hair and consoles me.

"Bella Blu, they are gonna be okay. I promise." As I stare up into those chocolate eyes, my tears continue to fall as I nod in agreement. Then, he kisses my forehead. Closing my eyes, I wait for it to be over, praying that when I open them that I'll see two people standing on the opposite side of the trestle alive and well.

With the train now in the distance, we step back on the trestle and make our way to the other side. With a well-lit sky from the full moon above, it's very easy to notice that there isn't a body on the other side, let alone two. Chase looks at me with fear in his eyes, and we follow the track across.

Once we reach the other side, panic sets in because they are nowhere to be found. Glancing both ways, we begin to yell for them, and after what feels like forever, we hear voices from below. Chase and I lean over the trestle and see them standing on bank soaking wet. Relief enters my body, and I begin to shake as happy tears begin flowing from my eyes.

Chase approaches me and pulls me in for comfort. When I finally get myself together, I look up at him and smile. "Thanks, Chase."

"You know I wouldn't have it any other way," he says as his eyes tell me so much more.

As I'm about to tell him the truth about what I want in life, Jake and Lyndsay appear on the trestle.

Running for them, I can't get there fast enough. Lyndsay and I meet and cry together. Then, Jake takes me in his arms.

"Thought that didn't happen often?" he questions.

"It doesn't. That has only happened to us one other time, but it's never been that close. I swear I was terrified when I couldn't see you. What if something would have happened to y'all?"

Taking my face in his hands, he responds, "There are no what if's. We are okay, and if anything, this has brought me back to reality." He places his forehead on mine.

"Um, I think it's time we get outta here," I say with everyone in agreement. We make our way back to the vehicles while the overwhelming feeling that something is different is definitely in the air.

"We'll see y'all tomorrow night at Joe's, right?" Lyndsay asks me as she eyes Jake.

"Yeah, but remember that we want to be incognito," I say in a questioning tone.

"We will do our best, but no promises," she says as she gets into her car and heads home.

Chase is still standing there as she leaves. "What was that?" he asks.

"I dunno, but you know Lynds."

"Exactly. I'll see y'all tomorrow. Just text me when y'all get there, and I'll let you in the back."

"Thanks, Chase," I say as I give him a hug goodbye, but hoping he understands why I'm thankful.

Jake and I make our way to the truck, and he opens my door like earlier tonight, but he's not the same as he was before the train. Once Chase is gone, I tell Jake to hold up a minute.

I slide onto the seat beside him and notice an unsure look in his eyes. "Jake, is everything okay? Really okay?"

Turning off the truck, he turns toward me. "Yeah, everything is just fine. Come here." He motions to me. I do as he says and come within inches of his godlike face.

"I'm here. Now what?" I say with a smirk, as there is no distance between the two of us.

"Do you know what I thought about when I saw the train coming?" I shake my head no because I am uncertain. "I thought about life, us, Lattimore, and what it would be like to never get on a stage again. I can't imagine not having any of that, but I will tell you what, I don't know what you would do without Chase and Lyndsay in your life. It's very evident that they mean more to you than you realize."

At this point, I'm unsure of what Jake is trying to tell me, but I'm pretty sure my heart already knows. He puts the truck in reverse, and we drive quietly back to the farm.

Chapter Six

As we drive back to the farm, it seems that I notice the little things that I love about this town, like the way one light is missing in The Depot sign, how you can always hear a cow mooing in the distance and the smell of country air.

Once we are back at the house, we make our way to the front porch. "Hey, Jake. Thanks for coming home with me," I say. He turns around and looks at me.

"Belle, this has been the best couple of days of my life. I always knew you were special, but now I realize why. You... Belle... are the real deal. You are what every guy dreams about. You take life by the horns and just live it. You have friends, family, and a support system that I can only dream about having."

"What do you mean? I thought your family was great." We turn and sit on the steps.

"My family is great, but they don't get it. My dad always wanted me to enlist, but that wasn't what I wanted. Music has been a part of my life since I can remember. I knew that someday it would be my life. They are proud of me, but my dream isn't my dad's. Sometimes I wish I could have been that person for him, but this is my dream. He's only been to one of my concerts since I started headlining. Mom, on the other hand, loves it, but she's kinda caught in between. She just tries to keep everyone happy. One time, she surprised me by showing up. Belle, it made my day. I think that's the best show I've ever had. Just be thankful you have your family's full support."

"What do you mean? Did something happen between you and your dad?" I ask.

Looking up into the sky, Jake replies, "Ever since I can remember we were told we would enlist, make him proud, and carry on the tradition. He always supported my music until he realized that was what I wanted for my future. He's proud of me, but his pride gets in the way."

Placing my hand on his lower back, I move in closer. "I wish there were something I could do to fix that, Jake. I couldn't imagine not having my family behind me one hundred percent. Please let me know if I can do anything for you. If you ever need someone to lean on, I'm here for you."

He lifts my chin for me to look into those baby blues, and then he brings his kissable lips to mine.

"Thank you, Belle. I knew the day I heard that sweet voice of yours on stage, it would be more than just a song. It's the sound of a relationship that will last an eternity." He brings his lips to mine again. The kisses are sweet, soft, and tender this time, almost as if he's trying to relay a message of what I really mean to him.

As headlights pull into the drive, we separate. Squinting, I notice that it's Beau. When he gets out, he joins us on the porch for a few minutes, noticing our wet clothes. He knows exactly what we have been up to.

"So, she made ya jump, huh?" Beau asks.

"Twice," Jake answers, and Beau seems confused.

"Um, there was a train comin'. Jake and Lynds had to jump," I say timidly.

"Dammit, Belle! That's why I always tried to keep you away. Wait. Where were you if he jumped with Lynds?"

Staring at the solid wood below my feet, I try to avoid this conversation. "I was talkin' to Chase. He got his panties in a wad, and I had to smooth things over."

He shakes his head. "When are you gonna grow up, Belle? You can't run after him every time he get's upset. You're not gonna be around forever." Ouch, that hurt.

"Shut up, Beau! You're just mad because I've made it out of this podunk town, and you haven't. You got so much talent it's ridiculous how you waste it around here!"

Jake looks at us like we are about to throw punches and then starts to laugh.

"What's so funny?" I ask.

"Y'all. It's like you're five or something. Cute, I'll tell ya... real cute. I'm gonna get outta these clothes," Jake says as he walks inside.

Turning toward Beau, I say, "You know, he's exactly right. We both need to grow the hell up." I go inside and head straight to my room to get ready for bed.

As I get ready, I let the events of the night replay through my brain. My emotions are a mess. Jake and I are taking things to a different level, and it's getting hot fast. Chase is telling me he doesn't want to be without me. Lyndsay is the same old Lynds, and Beau is my obnoxious older brother who will never change and will always wish he could be more like me. What a freakin' night.

After I finish getting ready for bed, I check on Jake. Walking next door, I knock gently before he answers for me to come in. As I enter the room, I notice he's standing there wearing only a pair of gym shorts and glistening from a fresh shower.

"Sorry about that, Jake," I say as I close the door.

"Come here," he says as we make our way to sit on the edge of his bed. "Look. I just had to get away from you two. Y'all are at each other's throats more than you realize. Be thankful you have Beau, but also remember that you're holding part of his dream. I wish there were a way we could make it a reality for him."

Stunned by what Jake just said, I decide to tell him my idea for Beau if I ever get to headline. "I've always wanted to take Beau with me on the road if I got my own tour. That way I'd always have family with me and help him live his dream as well."

Jake hovers over me and forces my body against the mattress. "That's the sweetest thing I've ever heard, but definitely not as sweet as you. You need to tell him that; he needs you to give him hope." His lips touch mine, and I begin to feel the heat rise once again. I beg for Jake to move closer, to make me feel him against me, and to cross the line of no return. Instead, he walks the line, pushes the limit, and makes me only crave him more.

"Belle, I want you. Don't think that I don't, but this isn't the place or time. You deserve so much more." Continuing to worship me, he trails soft kisses from my neck down my arm and to my hand, where he ends the kiss like only a prince would… or should I say… a country music god.

Chapter Seven

After pulling myself out of my country fairy tale, I leave Jake and go to my room, only to toss and turn for hours. My mind races to thoughts of Jake and me at the creek, Martin's, the trestle, and that bathroom, which is only inches away. What the hell am I doing?

Giving up on sleeping, I throw on a pair of cutoffs and tank top before making my way out to the tire swing out front. As I swing, I get lost in thought. My brain wonders to all the thoughts that had me tossing and turning. Ever since I can remember this is where I would go to clear my mind. It followed all the rules growing up, but felt like an escape.

As I swing higher and higher, I jump out of my skin when I hear Chase's voice. Glancing over my shoulder, I see him. "What the hell, Chase?" I inquire with a little anger in my voice.

"I just wondered if you were having the same problem I was having."

"And what would that be?" I ask like a smartass as I come to a complete stop on the swing.

Chase approaches me and begins to push me on the swing. As he pushes me, I relax and think about all the times we used to do this.

"The thought of you and me." Planting my bare feet on the ground, I abruptly halt myself mid-swing, jump up, and face Chase.

"No, that's not what I was thinkin' about! Not you and me! More like Jake and me!"

I can see the hurt in Chase's eyes and the anger bulging from his veins. As he gathers his thoughts, he doesn't look at me. Once he has his feelings and thoughts in check, he tells me exactly what he's thinking. "When are you going to wake up and realize that this is just a getaway for him, Bella Blu? Did you not see him checking out Lynds tonight? Lord only knows what happened when they jumped, if you know what I mean."

I take a step toward him to show him I'm not going to back down. "You asshole! Don't you dare say that! He's different. I know I shouldn't have crossed that line, but it's been crossed whether you like it or not," Then I back away and walk toward the house, leaving Chase standing there alone.

Once I'm in my bedroom, I glance out the window toward the swing. I see Chase sitting there, but not swinging. Not wanting to apologize, I crawl into bed, only to toss and turn even more than before. I shouldn't have said that to Chase. It was spiteful and not how I am. Letting my conscience get the best of me, I grab my phone, send him a quick text to tell him I'm sorry and hope he'll still save me a dance tomorrow night at Joe's. When he doesn't respond, a tear falls from my eye and eventually I drift off to sleep. Tonight has ended in disaster.

Chapter Eight

W aking up, i hear the tractor going in the distance and several people laughing and talking. What time is it? I peek at the clock and can hardly believe that it is almost noon. I never sleep this late. Feeling a little upset with myself, I jump up and throw on some old clothes. I had planned to help Daddy on the farm today. I figured that Jake might like to do a little farm work.

I stop by the guest room, and it's very evident that Jake isn't in here. Mama has brunch ready for me because breakfast is definitely over.

"Hey, honey! I saved you some, but you better be glad I did. Those men ate like a house full of teenage boys. I don't know what I would've done with a house full of those!"

Shaking my head, I take the plate, eat, and talk to Mama about everything.

"Bella, sweet girl. Let me tell you. Be careful whatever you do, but know that if you choose Jake, things will never be the same with Chase. He's always loved you. Beau will always support you, but it's been hard on him. He wants out, and I want to help him, but I don't know how."

"Mama, I have Beau covered. I haven't told him yet, but if I headline, he's going to work for me. It will open so many doors for him. I was really mean to him last night, though. Jake called us five-year-olds."

Mama laughs as she sets her coffee cup back down. "Y'all will always be that way."

"So, where is everyone?"

Mama points to the window, and I see Daddy, Beau, and Jake out in the field working together. I smile as I finish my food and then make my way outside.

"Somebody could've woken me, ya know? Someone needs to show you how to really do work on a farm," I tell Jake who is standing there in a pair of worn-out jeans and cutoff T-shirt that he must have borrowed from Beau. Damn, who thought my brother's clothes could look that good on someone.

"I think someone needed to rest up after a long night on the tire swing," Beau says, and I cut my eyes at him.

Jake looks at me inquisitively, and I tell him he doesn't wanna know.

Shaking it off, he goes back to working, and I join right in. After a couple of hours, we are all beat, and Mama has lunch ready. We go in and enjoy before going to finish one more task for Daddy.

"Hey, Jake. I gotta go check the fence out by the creek. You wanna go?" He gives me another curious look and smirks.

"Hell, yeah. I wanna go."

Loading up the Gator, we take anything we might need to repair a loose post or wire. It's an easy fix, especially with both of us working.

"Wanna go for a swim?" I wink.

"I thought you'd never ask," he says as he takes off his shirt and tosses it onto the Gator before removing his jeans. I know exactly what I'm about to do, but I decide to keep his curiosity at its pique as we make our way down to the creek.

Once we are there, I kick off my shoes, unbutton my shorts, and shimmy out of them while keeping one eye on Jake. Yeah, that was the right move. Then, I pull my tank top over my head and toss it onto the pile on the ground before jumping in.

As I surface, I'm met by another splash and automatically dragged underwater in one swift motion. When I reach the top, I find Jake with eyes full of passion.

"Belle, why'd you have to do that? Are you tryin' to kill me? I'm tryin' to be a good boy."

"Well, now, who said I wanted a good boy?" I ask as I disappear under the water and toward the rock island in the middle of the creek.

As I begin to crawl up the rock, Jake comes up behind me and pulls me back into the water. Falling backwards, I land right in his arms. He turns me around, pushes me up against the rock, and takes control like any good man would.

Chapter Nine

After jake and I have pushed every limit possible in the creek, we relax a few minutes as the sun starts to set in the sky.

"I guess we better get back. We've got a big night ahead of us tonight. I can only imagine what Cole's got planned."

"More like what Lyndsay and Chase have planned," Jake says. "You know they are the ones behind it."

"I know, but that's why I love them. They love me for me."

We climb out of the creek, and I put my clothes back on before we make our way to the Gator. Jake does the same once we reach it.

"I really hate that this is gonna end tomorrow," he says as fear runs through my veins.

"Whatcha mean?" I question.

"I just mean all of this," he replies as he points to the farm. "This has been the best break I've ever had… ever." He places his hand on my cheek. Not giving him a chance, I remove the space and place my lips on his and my arms around his neck. Once we finish, he starts to laugh.

"What's so funny?"

"You know we aren't gonna get anything done on tour now. We can't keep ourselves off each other."

"That's not a bad thing," I say as I make my way to the driver's seat. "Come on, music god. We've got places to go and people to sing our hearts to."

Once we are back at the house, we go our separate ways to get ready. Looking in my closet, I know exactly what I'm going to wear—a strapless cream-colored mini dress with a brown belt and a pair of Corral ladies Heart And Wing cowboy boots. Gazing into the mirror, I know that I need to wear my hair down. Once I'm finished, I stare back into the mirror, realizing how proud I am of myself. I have become the person I always dreamed of, and I have my friends and family to thank, but now I have someone that understands it as much as I do... Jake.

As I finish putting on the essential accessories, there's a brief knock at the door, and when I open it, I see Beau. He's not dressed for Joe's like I expected.

"Are you not goin'?" I ask.

"Nah. Y'all go have fun."

"Beau Bear! You have got to go!"

"Please tell me you didn't just pull the Beau Bear card?

Batting my eyelashes, I reply, "You bet your ass I just did!"

"Seriously? You want me to go with y'all tonight? I thought I might interfere with you two lovebirds." He sounds like the most annoying brother ever, but I must have the word 'guilty' written all over my face because he just smiles that I told you so smile.

"Not a damn word," I say, pointing my finger at him.

"Well, my only comment is this. He's a great guy, but he's not the one." I give him a look that could kill as he finishes his statement. "Have fun and enjoy life. You're living your dream. Don't let a guy hold you back, but if I were a bettin' man, I'd say you've already met your prince."

Turning around from Beau, I don't know what to say. I begin to question Jake and me, Chase and me, and the decisions I have made over the past few days.

"Belle, don't worry about what you do. I know you enough to know that you will make the right one when the time comes. I think Sarah and I might go, but you don't need us tagging along with y'all. We'll meet y'all there."

"Aight, Beau Bear," I say as I give him a hug. We might fight like we're five, but he's the best brother a girl could have, and one day I'm going to show him how important he is to me.

As Beau turns to leave, I know I need to tell him my thoughts. "Hey, Beau Bear?"

"Yeah?" he asks as he glances over his shoulder at the doorway.

"Um, I've been meanin' to tell ya. This headline thing. If it happens, I want you on the road with me."

His eyes get the size of grapefruits. "Huh? What are you talkin' 'bout?"

Making my way to him, I look him in the eye and tell him. "I want you to design my set and make sure everything goes like it's supposed to! I trust only you for that!"

"Really?!" he asks for reassurance. As I nod my head yeah, he takes me and picks me up and gives me the biggest Beau Bear hug of my life.

Once he puts me down, I grab my purse, and Beau and I make our way into the hallway. I stop mid-stride and gawk when I see the most beautiful man I've ever laid eyes upon. Closing the door to the guest room, I see Jake in a pair of Double "V" Straight Shooter jeans that I don't think I've ever seen an ass look that good in and a blue plaid pearl snap that is fitted in all the right places. He turns toward me and smiles that perfect half-grin that drives me and every other girl wild.

"Belle, you look fabulous," Jake says as he approaches me and kisses me on the cheek in front of Beau.

Not wasting another second, Beau takes his chance to leave. "Belle, we'll meet y'all there." I nod, and Beau makes his ways downstairs.

"You don't look so bad yourself," I say as I nudge him on the shoulder. "I don't know how we're gonna keep the barflies off ya."

"Real funny. I don't think I'll have to worry about that with you on my arm."

"Is that so, Mr. Bryant?"

"Yes, ma'am. I believe so. Now, let's go; honestly, I'm ready to enjoy a night out with a small stage."

"I couldn't agree more."

Mama and Daddy are getting ready to leave the house when we get downstairs.

"Well, look at y'all! If I didn't know better, I'd think y'all were hot country stars or somethin'," Mama says. "Y'all have fun, but be careful. We're going out with the Morgans tonight." She kisses me goodbye and hugs Jake. Daddy gives us a nod on the way out the door.

"You wanna eat here, or see what we can find on the way?" I ask.

"Oh, we're stoppin' on the way. I'd love to have a good burger."

I begin to cheese from ear to ear. "I think you just stole my heart! I know exactly where we need to go. Come on."

Closing the door behind us, we make our way to Jake's truck. I give him a one turn and stoplight direction to The Depot, home of the best burgers this side of Charlotte. Pulling into the parking lot, Jake looks uncertain. Placing my hand on his leg, I reassure him that this is the best burger joint around.

Once we are inside, we take the corner booth and order double bacon cheeseburgers, onion rings, and milkshakes. When the burgers arrive in front of us, my mouth begins to water just thinking about the taste explosion that is about to occur. Instead of digging in first, I watch Jake. The sound that escapes his mouth is damn near erotic.

He struggles for a napkin, and I help him out and wipe his mouth. "See. I told ya," I say with a wink.

"No wonder you lit up like a Christmas tree when I said 'burger'. We have got to bring the crew here on our way back to Nashville."

"Sounds good to me."

We finish eating and feel as full as a tick. "Ohmygosh, Jake! I don't know if I'm gonna be able to move when we get there."

"Oh I'm sure you will. I'm gonna make damn sure you're dancin' with me tonight."

Jake picks up the tab, and we make our way back to Charlotte. Once we are off I-85, I can't help but get excited. This is where my life changed, and it will always be like home to me.

As we make our way onto Wilkinson Boulevard, my heartbeat increases, and a smile spreads across my face. I can see the red neon light in the distance. Once we are there, we pull into the gravel parking lot, and I notice the line is not too long to get inside. Getting out my phone, I text Chase to let us in the back door anyway.

"Aight, Chase is gonna let us in around back."

Jake comes around and opens the door for me, but after closing the door, he pulls me into a strong embrace. He takes my soft blonde hair and places it behind my ear as he looks into my eyes.

"Belle, this is our night. Just us. Let's let loose and have some fun before we're back to reality." Biting my lip, I nod in agreement, and then his lips press against mine.

Taking me by the hand, we walk around back, and Chase is standing there in a pair of jeans and a black fitted tee with the Coyote Joe's logo in the corner.

"Well, if it's not the best thing I've seen all night!" Chase says with a wink, and I wrap my arms about him.

"You're not so bad yourself. I'm surprised you don't have to fight off the girls being all big and swollen in that shirt and all."

"Ah, you know you like it!"

"Eh, it's okay." I laugh, and we go inside.

Walking inside is like going back in time. The mechanical bull is to my right, and one drunk girl has already gotten enough liquid courage to ride it. The lights give an orange glow, and the bar in the middle is packed. As I glimpse over at the bar, I see Lyndsay. She throws her hand up, and the three of us walk that way.

Once Jake and I get a beer, Chase excuses himself to get back to work. We talk briefly before going to the dance floor. All the country line dancers we can stand greet us, and we join right in. Glancing over my shoulder, I laugh at the fact that no one has noticed us yet. When the song ends, I look to my right and see Cole.

"Cole!" I squeal as I head his direction. Jake and I talk to him a few minutes, and then Jake excuses us when he hears Brantley Gilbert's "Bottoms Up" coming from the house band. As we turn it up on the dance floor, things definitely heat up for the world to see.

Placing my arms around Jake's neck, my hips begin to sway to the music as we sing the lyrics together. As the chorus approaches, my hands move to his chest. After staring into his eyes, I turn around and show him everything about "Bottoms Up."

"Belle, you better stop because I'm about to take you out back and show you what you're doing to me."

"I dare you," I whisper. He takes me by the hand, and we start to make our way out when I hear Blake, the lead singer of the house band, say my name as the spotlight shines directly on me.

"Y'all put your hands together for our very own Belle Montgomery. Get your ass up here and show us what that big stage has done to ya!"

I let go of Jake, glance at Lyndsay and Chase, and make my way to the stage. Everything about this night feels right—being at Joe's with my friends, Jake, and living life to the fullest.

As I take the stage, the crowd goes crazy. The house band greets me with open arms, and I feel at home. I tell them I wanna go back in time by taking it back to when I used to do this regularly. Without mentioning the song, they take their places, and Zack, the drummer, counts five-six-seven-eight. The sound of Miranda Lambert's "Kerosene" begins to echo through the speakers, and I approach the microphone. Performing it like the first time I ever did on this stage, I sing with every ounce of my being. After a few other covers, I sing my new release, "Some Kinda Heartbreak." As I lose myself in the song, I can't help but relive the last time I stepped on this stage and who greeted me as soon as I got off it. Chase. I glance over and find him and Jake watching every move I make.

As I finish my last note, the light bulb goes off. I've got to get out of the past and into the future. I do the only thing that makes sense in the moment.

"How y'all doin' tonight? I'm so glad to be back home, but I've got a surprise. How many of y'all love Jake Bryant?" I can see Jake shaking his head no, but I don't care. It will be fun. "How'd you like to see us perform right here tonight for the first time together?" The crowd hoots and hollers. "Come on, Jake! For the crowd?" I say with my hands on my hips and my biggest pouty lips. He smiles and makes his way to the stage.

Jake takes a minute to talk to the band. He knows exactly what songs he wants to perform, including a duet with me that he says will make Chase smile. I know exactly what he means. Our song. It's one of the most famous duets in country music— "It's Your Love" by Tim and Faith. You'd think that this would make me happy, but instead, I'm the most anxious I have ever been in my life. Jake gives the crowd what they want by doing what he does best on stage. I step back out of the light and enjoy the view just like on tour. This time things are different. We are different. Different than we were a few hours ago. I feel like he's trying to prove himself against Chase, and I'm not sure how I feel about that.

Once Jake finishes his song, we join together for a fun duet of Sugarland's "Stuck Like Glue." As I turn and signal the band, the house lights focus on me. I begin to sing one of my favorite songs of all time. I zero in on Chase, and his face looks like he's seen a ghost when he peers into my eyes. I sing the verse straight to him.

People in the crowd find someone they love on the dance floor and sing as we do. Jake joins me at the chorus and sings his verse directly to me. I know I must be standing there with the goofiest grin as I join him in singing.

Out of the corner of my eye, I can see Chase at the bar, and the expression on his face hurts my heart. I've never wanted to hurt him in my entire life, but this is what I want. I want Jake Bryant, or at least I think I do.

Once the song ends, he pulls me in close and kisses my forehead. Forehead, really? I just knew he was going to tell the world about us tonight when he picked that song. Then, he asks me, "You think he liked it?" I feel a piece of my heart break when I see Chase slam his water and exit to the side porch. I wonder if this was Jake's way of making a point to Chase, and if so, we are done before things even get started.

As soon as the lights dim, I whisper to Jake, "You did that shit on purpose." Without thinking, I exit the stage and hurry to Chase.

When I walk outside, the cool air touches my sweaty skin and chill bumps instantly rise. Looking to my left and right, I start panicking to find him. I should have told him; that's what friends do. Now, there's nothing to tell. I don't want to be with someone that takes his power out on others, even if the world sees him as the best thing since sliced bread. I see him at the edge of the porch staring out into the grass.

I take a deep breath as I reach him. Placing my hand on his back, I don't say anything.

"Belle, you need to go. I can't do this here."

"Can't do what, Chase?"

Chase turns toward me with pain written all over his face. "Let you go. I can't let you go. You're everything to me and seeing you up there with him… singing our song together. I can't watch that."

"Chase, we have always been just friends."

"'Just friends'? I do believe there was one night that we were anything but 'just friends.'"

"Don't, Chase! Don't go there." Tears begin to form in my eyes.

"Bella Blu, that was our song, not y'alls. Tell me that it didn't feel the same. I saw the way you looked at me when you sang that first verse. You were singing to me. Then when you looked at him… I don't even want to talk about it. Please tell me it didn't feel like this." Chase takes me in his arms and pulls me into his perfectly chiseled body as his lips meet mine. They're soft at first and then harder with every moment. I try to resist him, but I can't. I've denied us as long as I can remember, and even though Jake has given me so much over the past few days, he's just a memory when Chase touches me. That spark I extinguished the night on the trestle is alive and burning tonight, and I won't put it out.

When we finally pull ourselves apart, I know I have to talk to Jake, but before I can do that, I have something that I must tell Chase.

"Chase, you know things will never be the same."

"Bella Blu, I don't want things to ever be the same. "

"I need to talk to him, even though I'm pretty sure he just won the Asshole of the Year award up there. I'd never do anything to hurt you and that hurt us both."

As I turn to make my way back inside, I'm met by Jake.

"Well, it appears like I was right all along, but the truth is this. Chase, I've known since the first time I met ya that she'd always choose you. I just wish I didn't have to do that for both of you to realize it."

"You did that on purpose? You weren't trying to rub it in Chase's face?" I ask.

"Damn right I did it on purpose. I've had the most fun in Lattimore, but the moment we stepped on that trestle, I knew I'd never win ya. Just thought I'd help y'all out. Now, if y'all don't mind, I'm gonna go talk to Lyndsay at the bar," he says with a wink.

"Jake Bryant, I just might have to drop that four-letter word again!"

"You wouldn't dare!" he says as he walks away.

Turning to face Chase, I fall into his arms. "So, maybe he doesn't take the Asshole of the Year award."

"No, he does, but you know that I'm never letting you go."

"I don't plan on ever being out of your sight."

Chase looks at me quizzically. "What do you mean? You have to leave tomorrow. What are you up to, Bella Blu?"

"I think I might need a bodyguard. You wanna go on the road with me?"

"As long as I get to stay on your bus and not Bryant's."

"I wouldn't have it any other way, Chase."

Placing my head on his chest, we sway to the sound of a country love song inside. Never in my wildest dreams did I plan on falling for my best friend, and I sure as hell didn't plan on Jake Bryant playing matchmaker.

About the Author

Casey Peeler grew up and still lives in North Carolina with her husband and daughter. Her first passion is teaching students with special needs. Over the years, she found her way to relax was in a good book.

After reading Their Eyes Were Watching God by Zora Neal Hurston her senior year of high school, she found a hidden love and appreciation for reading. Her perfect day consists of water, sand between her toes, a cold beverage, and a great book!

Connect with Casey
Facebook tumblr @AuthorCasey Goodreads Pinterest YouTube

www.ingramcontent.com/pod-product-compliance
Lightning Source LLC
Chambersburg PA
CBHW070355130626

46556CB00007B/3177

www.ingramcontent.com/pod-product-compliance
Lightning Source LLC
Chambersburg PA
CBHW070355130626
46556CB00007B/3177